CAN MAN

KILLER OF COP-KILLERS

BOOK ONE

A NOVELLA BY JOHN DITTO

First Edition: June 2018

ISBN: 978-1-7343501-2-8

Cover art copyright © by John Ditto
Editing by Faye Walker
Book Design by Elizabeth Domino

Acknowledgments

Denise Ditto Satterfield,
Author of *The Tooth Collector Fairies Series,* 2nd Place and Honorable Mention recipient of 2018 Purple Dragonfly Book Award

R.D. Vincent, Author of *Donbridge Series*

Police Officer Luke (Chad) Branton for buying the very first book of this series

Elizabeth Domino, Author, Blogger and last-minute procrastinator extraordinaire

Introduction

This novella I wrote is a story about a regular guy that has had terrible things happen to him. He fights back and is a hero to many. He has no super powers, but he has skills and unique ideas that enable him to do many good things in a violent way. He is a killer of cop killers...with a love story mixed in.

If you are looking for an easy read, this is it. I believe it's also perfect for reading if you are going on a road trip, train or plane ride. And after you finish it, you're going to want more. Don't worry, I'm working on the follow-up to this novella right now. Enjoy, and thanks for buying my novella.

Chapter One

As the blood worked its way down over the sweaty duct tape on the young cop's mouth, he looked up at his lanky tormentor and thought of his kids rather than his own life. The old brick warehouse was dark and vacant. Even if he could scream, there was no one to hear. He wondered how he had gone from kissing his beautiful wife goodbye that morning to being roped into an old heavy wooden chair on the third floor of a lunatic's torture chamber that night.

No questions, just pain. His fingers were broken and bent from the pliers. His face bloodied and his ears ringing from the hits of a small baseball bat like the kind you get as a souvenir at the ball game. Almost swollen-shut eyes looked up as a huge ball peen hammer was being raised over his head. A loud scraping noise came from the back wall of the warehouse. The tormentor swung around and squinted to see through the darkness. That third floor was empty, just like the rest of the six-story dilapidated building that should have been torn down years ago. The only things he could see were four old round metal trash cans against the distant wall. Satisfied it must have been a rat, he turned back around to his defenseless victim and remembered he was just about to crush his skull. But he decided to have another swig of his cheap whisky in the flask shaped bottle.

As he tilted his head back for a swallow, the noise happened again. Instantly, he spun around to look but saw nothing but trash cans. *Were there three or four trash cans before?* Laughing to himself he decided to take his last swig and crush this cop's head in. He emptied the bottle and raised the hammer. For a split second he thought he saw a brief shadow. Then he felt a slight pressure on his throat. Then a sting. Then a searing pain. A sheet of blood poured from his neck. His life slipped away. The lanky psycho slumped down, dead.

The cop looked up, squinting his swollen eyes. Just beyond the naked light bulb gently swinging, standing in the shadow was a dark figure wearing a large, round, flat metal head piece and a poncho made of metal slats. Puzzled but grateful, he nodded thanks to the stranger. The man was holding some sort of knife-like object that had just sliced a throat. Now it cut the ropes. The stranger pulled the tape away from the mouth of the thankful cop.

"You just saved my life. I don't know how to thank you." The stranger replied, "No, I'm thanking you."

Being able to breathe freely again, he asked, "Who are you...and what are you?"

After a few moments of silence, the reply came. "Remember how it went from four trash cans to three? And who am I? A killer of cop killers."

After the young cop bent over to free his legs with his mangled fingers, he raised back up to discover he was alone.

The agile stranger was already three buildings away. Wearing a poncho with metal slats and a large flat metal head piece was not something you could just walk down the street with. Over time, Jack Warren, aka "Can Man," had secured taut ropes from building top to building top. Walking tight ropes was something he learned as a boy. He was very good at it, even with the poncho.

Jack wore what surfers called booties on his feet. They were made of strong rubber sides with a hard rubber sole. The soles were flexible enough for his feet to make good contact with the taut ropes. They were silent as he traversed the tight ropes and silent when he was on the ground. Making no noise was imperative.

Getting around without being seen in the old warehouse district wasn't his best feat. Even with people looking right at him, he could hide in plain view. He did this by crouching down, pulling in the metal slats with unseen wires under the poncho. Then bringing his head down and the slats up till he looked like a silhouette of a trash can against an alley wall. He would leave a slit open so he could see everything. The lid was secured on his head with straps. So even if someone tried to open the trash can, it would just appear to be stuck on securely.

At the hospital emergency room, the young cop was receiving medical care and telling his story to his sergeant, Sergeant Mike, and about a half-dozen other police officers.

"This guy absolutely saved my life. I don't know where he came from. There were only three or four trash cans on that entire floor."

His burly sergeant asked, "Three or four trash cans? You're a cop. You are supposed to notice everything. Was it three or four?"

Chris, the young cop, looked down and closed his swollen eyes. "Sarg, I'm not sure because even the perp said it changed from four to three."

"Okay, maybe that's where your rescuer came from."

All the cops looked at each other and one mumbled, "This guy hides looking like a trash can."

An older overweight cop laughed and said, "That's the most ridiculous thing I've ever heard."

His Sarg looked at him and barked, "Officer Gorby, you got a better explanation?"

Officer Gorby cleared his throat and replied, "No, sir."

After some silence Sergeant Mike said, "It seems we have a guy who can hide in plain sight and protects cops while the cops are protecting the public. Okay boys, I've never had this kind of situation before. We got a killer who protects cops."

Officer Gorby asked, "Are we supposed to concentrate on catching this guy over everything else?"

"No," Sergeant Mike said in a hushed tone. After a few moments of silence, the Sarg looked into each of the officers' eyes and said, "One more thing. I better never hear any of you talk about this Can Man. I have my reasons. You hear me!" All six officers nodded yes. The truth was Sergeant Mike had a pretty good idea who this Can Man was. He had his reasons to leave it alone. He said, "Okay men. Let's get back to the station and back to work."

Chapter Two

The sun had already been up for hours when Jack Warren opened his eyes. One of the benefits of owning a local pub was you didn't have to get up early.

Suzanna's Pub was the name he'd given it, in honor of his murdered wife.

Jack had once been the happiest guy on earth. He married his high school sweetheart. Suzanna was on the drill team. She always loved dancing, even as a little girl. She would jump up in front of the TV and start dancing. The more people watching, the better. She was a good athlete, but dancing on the drill team was perfect for her. It gave her an audience of hundreds. The half-time show was never long enough for her. She loved it.

Jack had held high hopes of playing professional baseball. He played first base. He liked that position because he was involved in just about every hit. His batting average was always in the 300's, which meant he got a hit about once every three times. He was always hoping a scout would discover him, but it was not to be.

Jack's blue-collar family was hard-working. His older brother, Larry, joined the Navy. That was the only way he was ever going to travel and see the world. He could learn a skill, too. Their dad was also in the Navy. Jack's dad used to tell him and his brother a lot of stories when they were little about his time spent on that aircraft carrier. At first, he was assigned below deck moving tons of supplies around with a forklift. His dad didn't join the Navy to be a fork lift driver, so he went to training classes on board to get a job on the deck.

After watching the sailors doing their parts to get the fighter jets off and on the deck, Jack's dad, Derrek, decided he wanted to be one of those guys with the paddles. They would motion to the pilots regarding take-offs. It was loud and exciting for Derrek. No more driving a fork lift below deck. He was in the sunshine and fresh air, having the time of his life.

Sadly though, Derrek came down with bladder cancer. The doctors told him it was because of his heavy smoking. Derrek passed away and left Jack, Larry and their mom on their own. Jack's dreams of playing professional baseball were dashed. He worked two jobs to help his mom.

Jack was very athletic and that's what caught Suzanna's eye. The two of them hit it off big. When they were together, everyone else became invisible. Her parents weren't too excited about the relationship. They were considered upper middle class and Jack was blue collar. Suzanna's dad was a senior vice president at one of the biggest banks in the southwest. He was also a partner in a home construction company. They had a huge home with a pool and, of course, new cars.

Jack wasn't envious of her family's wealth. He knew her dad worked long hours to earn everything they had. Suzanna saw that Jack was down to earth. That made her love him even more. Her mom also saw that in Jack and liked him. Suzanna's dad wished she could have fallen in love with a better-off guy but that wasn't the way love worked. Her dad told her mom that as long as she was happy with a good, decent man - that was the most important thing. They gave their blessings to Suzanna.

Back then Jack's face hurt because he smiled so much. Suzanna made him laugh all the time. And when he held her in his arms and asked her, "What happens if I don't let go?" she would laugh and say, "I don't know, let's find out!"

Jack opened a small flower shop partly because Suzanna loved flowers and partly because Jack always enjoyed gardening. Even as a child, he had taken some beans from the kitchen and planted them on the side of their house. His mom discovered Jack's garden and encouraged him to keep it up. She would give him other types of beans to plant. Then little Jack got some flower seeds and started growing flowers to give to his mom.

After a couple of years of marriage, Jack and Suzanna started to talk about having a family. It didn't take long before Suzanna was with child, or should I say children – twins – a boy for him and a girl for her. Jack couldn't believe his good fortune.

Five months into her pregnancy, Suzanne was at the bank to ask about starting a savings plan for her soon-to-come little ones. While she was sitting at a desk off to the side of the lobby, three thugs burst into the bank, shouting, and fired a shotgun into the air.

The noise was so loud because of the thick walls and confined space. Plaster and dust dropped from the ceiling. A few women were screaming. Everyone hit the floor.

The pot-bellied leader yelled, "This is a bank robbery. Stay on the floor, shut up, and you will get out of this alive."

The teller furthest from the front door hit the panic button as soon as the thugs came in. Two of the bad guys had already jumped the counter and were robbing the tellers of their cash. Unknown to them, there were two cop cars just blocks away. When the call went out, *armed robbery in progress,* Officer Jim Stevens turned on his lights but not his siren. He got there in seconds. He knew the bank well. He also knew the code to enter from the back door.

Officer Stevens radioed dispatch and told them he was going into the back of the bank.

The other officer, Bob Taylor, just pulled up to the bank front. Officer Taylor knew after twenty-one years on the force that it's never easy when you have the public in a possible cross fire.

As Officer Stevens entered the back of the bank, he could see customers on the floor and one big guy with a shotgun standing in the middle of the bank lobby. He saw movement of the other two thugs working their way from teller to teller. As Officer Taylor entered the front door, the leader had his back to the veteran officer. Taylor raised his 45-caliber pistol and took aim at his target, which was only about twenty feet away. He yelled, "Drop it and turn around with your hands up!"

The surprised thug spun around with the shotgun. Officer Taylor knew with his many years on the force that sometimes these guys would rather die than go back to prison. Without any hesitation, Taylor pulled his trigger and moved after every shot. The leader was shot three times before hitting the floor and never got a shot off. Meanwhile, the other two-armed robbers had their pistols pulled and were desperately looking for an escape route. Running towards the back of the bank away from Officer Taylor, they ran into Officer Stevens.

Afraid for her unborn babies, Suzanna had jumped up to run out the back of the bank. Officer Stevens lunged out from behind the corner wall and placed himself between the bad guys and Suzanna. Many shots were fired by the thugs and several hit the young mother to be. Officer Stevens had his vest on, but one deadly bullet found his neck just above the vest. Officer Taylor had his pistol aimed at the two fleeing criminals. When they opened fire on Officer Stevens, Officer Taylor opened fire on them. He had four bullets remaining and shot each one twice, killing both last two bank robbers. He rushed to Suzanna and Officer Stevens, but they were both gone. All he could do was put his head down. Outside the bank were sounds of sirens approaching from all directions.

Officer Taylor told the story to Jack about how Officer Stevens gave his life trying to protect his pregnant wife from the bank robber's bullets. He literally died lying in front of Suzanna. It was the most heroic thing Officer Taylor had ever seen. Every heart-breaking emotion went through Jack's mind. He didn't know if he could go on living without his wife Suzanna and his unborn family. Weeks went by without him opening the flower shop. He just stayed home in the darkness.

One morning Jack decided he must get up. It's what Suzanna would have wanted. He started thinking about the young cop, Officer Stevens. That guy didn't know Suzanna, yet he gave his life to protect her. That was so huge. It was the noblest thing a human being could do. That's when Jack decided he was going to return the favor in a big way. And how could he do that? He was going to become a killer of cop killers.

Chapter Three

Jack's plan required a lot of thought. First was how not to get caught. Hiding in plain sight made sense. Jack remembered playing hide-and-seek as a child. One night when he was about to get caught he crouched down and brought in his arms and legs. At a distance, his silhouette looked like a big bag sitting on the ground next to a wall. His friend looked right at him and then walked on by. It worked!

Jack continued thinking about this until he had a brilliant idea. After much practice, and some trial and error, he came up with the trash can disguise – a poncho with metal slats and a wide-rimmed metal hat. He added a black pull-over ski mask to hide his face. Second was how to get around without detection? He secured a tight rope from the roof top of the five-story building he lived in to the six-story building across the street. Night after night he practiced walking back and forth across the taut rope. Every night or so he connected another building to his network until soon he could get all around town without ever touching the ground.

Third, he needed to figure out how to stay informed on police activity and especially getting info on cop killers. The best place for that was from the cops themselves – but you just can't go up to the police and ask. He thought if he could be around off duty cops, he could listen in. Owning a pub cops frequented would be perfect.

And fourth was how to end the lives of the stains on civilization, cop killers. It had to be quiet. No gun shots. He thought about a stabbing knife, but how many times would it take? Suppose it turned into a big struggle? Lots of variables. So, he ruled that out.

Jack's early life he spent summers working on a hog farm just outside of town. He was not from a wealthy family and always needed money. On that farm Jack learned how to cut the throats of hogs being slaughtered. At first it was creepy but after several summers it became second nature.

Now, all he had to do was switch out his skills from hogs to cop killers. This was a perfect fit. Quiet, and a way to get close to his victims.

Back then, Jack had an Uncle Tito who was a metal smith. He was talking to Tito one day and said, "I wish I could have a better knife for slitting hog throats. The one they gave me to use gets slippery from blood and becomes a problem."

Tito asked, "What are you thinking?"

Jack thought for a few moments and muttered, "I would really like a blade that curves around like a sickle. Like the kind you see on a Russian flag. But not that big and the arc not that pronounced. About half the size of a real sickle. Gentler arc and some finger holes." The hog's blood made the handle slippery, so finger holes in the handle would make for a sure grip.

Tito always loved a new challenge and told Jack that he would make him one. Weeks later, Tito surprised Jack with his new creation. It was the most beautiful thing Jack had ever seen. It was made with several hard and soft metals - razor sharp with a stainless-steel blade and a slight arc. Perfect for reaching under a hog's throat. The handle was ribbed brass. It was like a set of brass knuckles were incorporated into the handle. The two different colored metals were married at the base of the blade. It met and exceeded Jack's expectations. It even had a textured thumb rest at the top of the handle. It was truly a work of art. Jack asked, "How can I ever repay you Uncle Tito? I have no money to spare."

Tito said, "I know cash is short. That's why you work your butt off. How about some sausage and bacon?"

Jack laughed and said, "That I got! And it's coming from the first hog I slaughter with this new blade."

Now, all the pieces were in place. His deep loss of Suzanna and unborn babies would never go away, but eliminating the scumbag killers on the streets seemed to be the least he could do.

He sold the flower shop. He searched near the police station for a space to lease where he could open a new pub. As an incentive, he got the word out that every cop who came into the pub would get his or her second beer on the house. This was an unwritten rule. The local police loved it. Jack hired a couple of cute waitresses while he bartended. He quickly became good friends with many, many cops. Even cops from other nearby stations started frequenting Suzanna's Pub.

They knew about the loss of his wife and their fellow officer Stevens who died trying to shield her from the flying bullets. They considered Jack one of them.

Cop killers are not common. They are a special breed of killer. Killing an unarmed man or woman is a lot easier than killing an armed and trained officer. Not to mention all of his backup. So, lots of time passed without any cop killers active in their city.

It was about a year later when Jack overheard that someone tried to kill a cop with a machete. It was an ambush on a street patrol officer walking downtown.

Officer Garza regularly walked the retail businesses at night, checking to make sure that their doors were shut and locked. Garza also looked for movement in the shops. He took great pride in protecting those businesses. The way he saw it they paid taxes and that's how he got paid.

Late one evening, about 2:30 in the morning, Officer Garza was walking his regular beat. It was very quiet, as usual, and that's the way he liked it. While he waited on the corner for the traffic light to change, he felt a great impact on top of his left shoulder. The heavy uniform shirt gave him some protection, as well as the shoulder strap of his bullet proof vest. But the impact of the large blade broke his collar bone and his attacker wasn't through yet.

Officer Garza reeled from the first hit. The long blade came down again and again. His hands, forearm and shoulders were bleeding profusely. His screams were heard by an off-duty security guard. At a full run and still over a block away, he pulled his pistol and began shooting in the air. This was enough to get the attacker to stop chopping at Officer Garza and make a run for it. The security guard reached the wounded cop and pulled out his phone and dialed 911. Soon the night air was filled with sirens and flashing lights.

Later at the hospital, two detectives were debriefing Officer Garza. "Can you tell us about the attacker? What did he look like? Did he say anything?"

These were the usual questions that Officer Garza had asked victims himself. All he could remember was the guy was yelling at him in Spanish. Garza was fluent in Spanish but said it wasn't Mexican. It was a different dialect of Spanish. Sadly, he didn't get a good look at the guy because it was dark. The surprise attack came from behind. He was just trying to stay alive. He didn't have a chance to pull his revolver before shots rang out and the attacker fled.

Back at his pub, Jack heard all of this and more. He listened for any details that might help him find this guy before they could make the arrest. This attacker sounded like he was emotionally involved. After all, if he just hated cops, he could just as easily shoot the cop in the head from behind – sneak attack. But this business of trying to kill a cop with a machete was up close and personal.

Officer Garza said, "His words were in Spanish, but not Mexican. He didn't roll his R's. This is typical of Caribbean Hispanics."

Something else appeared strange about the attack. Garza said it was a machete striking him. As everyone knows, a machete has a long smooth blade. Garza's wounds had a stabbing look to them. So how could a machete blade have a bit of a stabbing effect? Jack got online and researched machete blades. Sure enough, he found one. It was called a brush machete with a dull upward protrusion at the end of the blade.

Jack continued to listen without overtly appearing to be eavesdropping. Officer Garza said he used the word *pare* instead of the Mexican word *alto*. Jack knew from a visit to Puerto Rico that the stop signs had *pare* on them instead of *alto*.

So, he thought the attacker might have been Puerto Rican. Garza also said the guy was probably young, maybe in his twenties. How else could a guy do a full sprint for blocks, fleeing the scene?

Jack started mentally putting together a profile of the attempted cop killer. *Okay, let's see*, he thought. *This attacker is a young male, probably in his twenties, Puerto Rican and has a specific grudge with the local police.*

That eliminated a whole lot of people but still left a lot. Jack decided the killer must have had a run-in with the law one way or another. Something happened that made this guy snap and try to kill a cop. But was it just any cop, or was it Garza?

The next morning, Jack got up early to get online and research newspaper articles. He looked for anything that had Officer Garza's name and for any incidents that had Puerto Ricans involved. He found nothing.

Weeks went by with no new news. Jack was at his pub one Monday morning to receive another weekly beer delivery. He was doing some paperwork on the bar. He wasn't open till noon and it was only 10:30.

The regular delivery guy was bringing in tall stacks of beer cases on his dolly. He always had the same delivery person, Jose, a good guy.

Jack looked up from his bill paying. He knew this was a crazy long shot but asked anyway. "Jose, where are you from?"

Jose stopped, looked up and said, "Mister Jack, I was born in Mexico City."

Jack said, "Oh, okay," and went back to his paperwork.

Jose took a load of beer cases to the walk-in cooler. Coming back through with his empty dolly, he stopped and said to Jack, "But I grew up in Puerto Rico."

Jack dropped his pen.

Chapter Four

Jose leaned on his tall, empty dolly and began telling Jack about the move his family made to Puerto Rico from Mexico when he was only two. Jose's dad had a brother in San Juan who had a delivery service company, and he offered Jose's dad a job. They moved there for a better life.

Growing up, Jose spoke Puerto Rican instead of Mexican although both were very similar. As Jose was talking, Jack thought that even though Jose fit Officer Garza's description of his attacker, Jose had no motive and seemed to be a hardworking, honest guy.

He went on to talk about his cousin he grew up with, Ray Ray.

Unlike Jose, Ray Ray was always getting into trouble. At first it was little things like lying about stuff, stealing bicycles, or anything that caught his eye. He barely passed in school, had no interests in sports, and was always starting fights. When he would get suspended from school, he was happy.

When both boys turned thirteen, they got a job chopping sugarcane in Puerto Rico. It paid very little and often Jose showed up and Ray Ray was a no-show. The company gave each of them a machete to cut sugarcane and deducted the cost from their first pay check.

Jack looked up and asked Jose, "You both had machetes? So, did they have a long sharp blade?"

Jose laughed and said, "Of course, Mister Jack. That's what a machete looks like."

"Okay," Jack laughed. Jose leaned on his dolly back and was about to leave when he muttered, "Ray Ray got the fancy machete. The one with the big head."

Jack's attention immediately zeroed in on every word Jose said. "What do you mean, big head?"

Jose explained machetes have many uses – from cutting coconuts out of treetops to cutting up a juicy pineapple.

Jack asked again, only with more seriousness, "What about the big head?"

Jose explained, "A machete with the big head is for cutting sugarcane or anything you want to cut down. And it has a piece that sticks out."

Jose said, "I really have to go. Many other bars owners are waiting and looking out of their windows for me. Ha-ha. See you next week, Mister Jack." The door shut and the little customer bell on top rang.

Jack thought about the new info. *Could Ray Ray be Officer Garza's attacker? Age is right. Check. Speaks Puerto Rican. Check. Owns a bush machete. Check. Or at least he used to. I'll have to find that out.*

Jose said Ray Ray was always in trouble. Maybe as an adult he had graduated into the big time. Cop killer!

Jack needed more info on Ray Ray. Had he had any run-ins with the law? Or more specifically, any run-ins with Officer Garza? He needed Ray Ray's last name to do some research, so he called his beer distributor.

The lady on the other end said, "Golden Beverage Delivery. How may I help you?"

Jack cleared his throat and thought quickly. *How do I get Jose's last name?* "My name is Jack Warren and I own Suzanna's Pub."

"Oh yes, Mr. Warren. How are you?"

Jack was a little relieved at the welcoming response. "Your delivery man, Jose, just left and..."

The lady's voice interrupted Jack and asked, "Is everything okay? Was the delivery wrong?"

Jack laughed and assured her, "No, no everything is just fine. As a matter of fact, that's why I'm calling."

The lady said, "Oh?"

"Yes, Jose is an excellent delivery man and I wanted to write a letter to the owner of your company. I just wanted to let him know that as far as I'm concerned, I couldn't ask for a better delivery man. I was wondering if I could get his last name to make sure the credit gets to the right Jose, in case you have more than one."

She laughed and said, "As a matter of fact, we have three Jose's. His last name is Latoni."

Jack got the correct spelling and thanked her for her help.

"I hear you have another call coming in, so I won't take up anymore of your time."

"No problem," she cheerfully responded.

Jack couldn't resist asking one more important question. "Is Ray Ray's last name also Latoni?"

"Why, yes, it is. Gotta go now. Thanks for calling."

Jack got a ton of info from that call. But first things first. He got a sheet of paper and wrote a sterling approval letter for Jose and decided to also include a bit of praise for the friendly informative receptionist. He got their address off the beer delivery invoice and put the letter in the mail.

Jack turned his attention back to his real concern. Was Ray Ray the attacker of Officer Garza? The only way to learn more was to listen more. He knew the local cops would start coming in around 5:00.

Jack went about getting the bar all stocked and cleaned up before the after-work customers arrived. He was thinking about his two waitresses. They also hear the cops talking amongst themselves. He would love to hear what they hear. But he just couldn't say, "Okay girls, as you know I am a killer of cop killers and I need you to listen and find out more info on Garza's attacker."

Jack thought, *Mouth closed, ears open.* Besides, he didn't want to involve his waitresses in the Can Man nocturnal activities. All in all, he felt pretty good about the info he had already obtained.

Around 4:30, a couple of the big shots at the police department came in. They liked to get there early so they could get their favorite two seats at the bar - right in front of the flat screen TV. Jack always left it on a sports channel. He said hello and got their favorite two draft beers. Stepping slightly away from the bar and pretending to watch the TV, he wiped down beer mugs. But what he really was doing was keeping his mouth shut and listening.

Police Chief Dickens and Sergeant Mike were talking about the usual stuff, wife, kids and some sports talk. Jack wanted to ask, "Don't you guys want to talk about what you have on Officer Garza's attacker?" But of course, that's not the way it works.

About an hour went by and more officers started arriving. Some grabbed a stool at the bar and some went to the tables. Both the police chief and Sergeant Mike paid their tab and said, "See you next time, Jack." And they were gone.

Jack worked his way up and down the bar, listening a bit to each conversation, and removing empty glasses. No one was talking about Garza's attack. He even came out from behind the bar to pick up glasses and wipe down tables, trying to listen in, but no one said anything of importance.

Day after day, the same thing. Towards the end of the week, Officer Garza came in. Everyone was so happy to see him. He still had some bandages and some stitches. Garza told everyone, "I'd much rather look at all of your ugly mugs than those nurses with those hypodermic needles."

Everyone laughed, and Officer Taylor patted him on the back.

"Ouch," hollered Garza. "Take it easy. I've still got stitches on top of my shoulders."

"Sorry," Officer Taylor said. "We are all just happy to see your cranky butt." They all laughed.

Jack announced, "Officer Garza's beers are on the house." A small round of applause filled the air. "Till Christmas!" The applause was much louder.

Once again Jack went into listening mode. Garza was asked a few questions about his attack, but what he said Jack already knew. The more he thought about it the more he realized how far ahead he was of their investigation.

Chapter 5

On Monday morning Jack rolled out of bed thinking it was time to talk some more to Jose. See if he could find out more about Ray Ray. Preferably if there was a connection to Officer Garza.

Jack knew he had to be nonchalant about gathering information. He couldn't just ask a lot about Ray Ray and the next thing you know, the guy's dead.

Later that morning Jack was at his bar doing his weekly receipts when he saw Jose pull up in his delivery truck. He got his dolly out, threw open the sliding side doors and began stacking cases of beer. Jack watched him and thought,

I'm going to pretend to be real interested in this bookkeeping.

Jose pushed open the door and walked in with his dolly stacked high without looking up. Jack announced, "Hello, Jose." The next thing Jack knew, Jose set down his dolly and rushed over to Jack and was shaking his hand.

Surprised, Jack looked at Jose and asked, "What's going on?"

With a gigantic smile, Jose said, "Thank you, Mister Jack, for writing that beautiful letter to my company."

"Oh yeah," Jack nodded. The truth was he had already forgotten about it. "They gave me a nice raise and even gave me another week of paid vacation."

Jose could not be happier.

Jack smiled back. "Jose, you've earned it. You're always on time and never get the order wrong."

"Thank you, thank you, thank you," Jose exclaimed.

Jack said less and listened more. That was his mantra. He needed to learn more about Ray Ray. As Jose was going back and forth to the cooler, Jack was wondering how to bring up

Ray Ray without looking obvious. Then as fate would have it, Jose stopped to chat a moment with Jack before he left.

"Mister Jack, I wanted to tell you that our receptionist, Heather, also got a raise because she was praised in your letter."

"Wow," Jack replied. "Your company seems to be a very appreciative place to work. I'm glad they're taking care of you."

Jose made his way back to his delivery truck, loaded the dolly and drove off. Jack looked down at his paperwork but didn't see it. He was busy thinking about Heather. She might know some information on Ray Ray that could shed some light on a connection to Officer Garza.

A few days went by. Jack was in the bar when the phone rang. As Jack picked up the phone he looked at the clock. It was almost 11:00 in the morning. "Suzanna's Pub, may I help you?"

The female voice asked, "Is this Jack Warren?" "Yes, it is. What can I do for you?"

The lady sounded a little shy. "This is Heather with Golden Beverage Delivery." Jack said, "Oh, hello. Is everything okay?"

She quickly answered, "Yes, everything is okay. Everything is better than okay. Thanks to your letter, I got a raise and I wanted to stop by your pub and meet you and personally thank you."

"Oh, Okay. That sounds great," Jack said.

"How about this Friday around 5:30?" Heather suggested.

Jack laughed. "I hope you like cops, because this is kind of their hangout and it's probably the safest place in town."

Heather giggled. "Great, I'll see you Friday."

Jack hung up the phone and thought this could be the break he'd been waiting for. He looked down at all the bills and thought to himself, *I can't even think about this stuff right now.* He pulled open a drawer and tossed them in there for later.

He was too excited to think about anything else right now. Wiping the bar down was about all he could do.

All these thoughts were racing through his head. *How to find out more about Ray Ray? Was there a run in with Officer Garza? Would Heather be willing to talk about stuff like that with a customer?*

And he had to do all of this without looking suspicious. Not to mention, being interested in whatever she wanted to talk about. He needed to calm himself down.

The clock seemed to have slowed down. He found himself checking it a lot.

Would Friday ever get here?

Chapter 6

Finally, it was Friday morning. Jack jumped out of bed and into the shower. He found himself dressing a little nicer. Crisp dry-cleaned shirt and slacks. He even shined his shoes and thought, *I think this is the first time I've ever shined these shoes*. Thursday, he had gotten a haircut and even a manicure. He hadn't been this excited in a long time. When he got to his pub, he started really cleaning everything good. He wiped all the bottles lined up on top of the cabinets that displayed his beers on hand. Jack kept looking at the old-timey clock on the wall even though he told himself to stop looking at the time.

Jack looked up when he heard the bell at the front door ring. "Hey, Jack." It was Sergeant Mike and Officer Gorby.

"It's about time you guys got here," Jack said. He looked at the clock. It was 5:00.

Three more cops came in, followed by Chief Dickens. The Chief joined Officers Gorby and Mike at the bar. Jack gave another quick look at the clock and saw he had about fifteen minutes before Heather arrived.

Everybody had their beers and Jack went to the restroom to wash his hands and make sure he hadn't spilled something on his shirt. As he looked in the mirror he surmised that he looked fine and said to his own reflection, "I can do this."

When he stepped out of the restroom, he noticed that his waitress, Jolene, had arrived and was behind the bar and filling a couple of draft beer mugs for two cops that had come in minutes before. Jack looked up at the clock and saw it was 5:32. He thought, *where could she be?* Then he made fun of himself and thought, *Geez, give her a chance to find a parking place*.

He calmed himself down and went back behind the bar and thanked Jolene for covering for him. She said, "No problem," smiled at him, got her tray and went out to the tables to check on the customers.

Jack had his back to the door when Heather arrived. She scanned the pub and figured that Jack had to be the one behind the bar.

Walking up to an empty bar stool, she sat down right behind Jack, and announced, "Hey sailor, want some company?"

He spun around and saw a woman that took his breath away. Heather had shoulder-length light brown hair with strawberry blond streaks, with freckles across her nose and cheeks and the brightest emerald eyes he had ever seen.

He suddenly realized he needed to speak. "I'm not a sailor, but I'd love some company."

She laughed and said, "I'm Heather and I hope you're Jack."

He said, "Don't worry. I'm so glad to finally meet you." They shook hands across the bar. He wanted to talk to her where it was a little more private.

"Jolene, could you come over here and watch the bar for a few minutes," Jack said.

She said, "No problem," like she always did.

Jack heard the bell on the front door again. It was Betsy, his other waitress. Now he could talk privately with Heather and see if she knew of a connection between Ray Ray and Officer Garza.

"Heather, follow me over here to a table where we can talk more privately," Jack said.

Betsy came over and, looking at Heather, she said, "Can I get you a drink?" Heather said, "Yes, a house Chardonnay would be fine."

Jack looked up at Betsy and said, "Make that two."

Betsy looked at Jack, a little puzzled because she had never seen Jack drink wine before. She took the order and said, "I'll be right back."

Jack turned his attention back to those distracting green eyes. "I have to ask, are those really your natural colored eyes or are you wearing some of those fancy colored contact lenses?"

Heather smiled and said, "Yes, these are my natural color. And don't worry, I get asked all the time."

They talked about all the usual stuff new acquaintances talk about. Where are you from, work, growing up – the usual. Turns out Heather had a husband that was killed two years earlier by a drunk teenage driver running from the cops in his dad's car that he wasn't supposed to be driving and broad-sided her husband's car, killing him instantly. She had no children but wanted a family someday. Jack told her he was sad that happened to her.

Then she looked into his eyes and said, "So what's your story?"

He told her that he too had lost his spouse. She was accidentally caught in a cross fire during a bank robbery. His wife and a police officer were killed and that's why he opened this pub where the police come.

Heather looked at Jack and asked, "How do you get the police to come here?"

"Well, that was easy. I give them their second beer free. It's an unwritten rule here."

Heather laughed, "That's very smart, and you are a good person." The two talked for a while and ordered more wine. Jack told Betsy to just bring a bottle.

Once again, she looked at Jack, puzzled, smiled and said, "Be right back."

Jack knew he needed to get back to getting information. He started talking about Jose and hoped she would bring up Ray Ray at some point. That didn't happen, so he brought it up himself. "Jose is as solid as they come but what's up with his cousin?"

Heather said, "Jose is the best employee we have, and yet his cousin is the worst." They both agreed that it never makes any sense.

Jack took a deep breath and asked, "I know it's none of my business, but do you know if Ray Ray has ever been in trouble with the law?"

Heather responded, "Don't worry. That's a legitimate question." She looked around at all the cops in there, leaned forward and whispered, "I think he got in trouble dealing drugs."

Jack thought that a lot of people get in trouble with drugs. But he was looking for a Garza connection. This was something Heather couldn't provide. After her third glass of wine, she told Jack that she needed to get going and told him what a pleasure it was to meet him and thanked Jack for the kind letter he wrote to her company.

He walked Heather to her car and said to her as she got in, "I was wondering if it would be okay to give you a call?"

She looked up at him with those beautiful green eyes and said, "I was hoping you would."

She put her hand on top of his and said, "I'm so glad I met you, and thanks for all the good things you do."

As she drove off, Jack had a conflict going on. He thought, *Am I more interested in Heather or getting to Ray Ray?* He had to admit Heather had stirred some feelings he hadn't felt since Suzanna was murdered. As he walked back to the pub, he thought, *Suzanna's murder.* Those two words brought him back to Ray Ray. He hadn't found a connection to Officer Garza, but he had learned that Ray Ray had a run in with the law over drugs.

Back in the pub, Jack was eavesdropping on Sergeant Mike when he heard something curious. Sergeant Mike was telling Chief Dickens that he had heard some scuttlebutt that Officer Garza was taking bribes from drug dealers on his beat and went on to say that he didn't believe a word of it. Jack thought, *Hmmm. I wonder if it's possible that Ray Ray was bribing Officer Garza to let him do his drug sales. Maybe something happened between those two. Maybe Garza wanted more money.* Jack needed to be sure before he put on the Can Man outfit and did what Can Man does, kills cop killers.

After a few weeks and a couple of dates, Jack and Heather's bond was growing. They kept having these funny little things come up that made them laugh. Later it would become their own little inside joke. One day Jack was reminiscing about his flower shop. Heather said she really loved it when hummingbirds came around.

Jack said, "Do hummingbirds really hum?"

Heather looked at him, scrunched her shoulders and went *hummm*. So, from then on when he would ask her a question, she would scrunch her shoulders and go *hummm*.

Chapter 7

Heather was visiting Jack's pub one day after work when Jack told her that the Police Department was having their annual BBQ at the city park and was wondering if she could go with him. They considered Jack one of them. Heather of course said yes. It was on a Saturday and she was off weekends. The park had a small lake and lots of big trees. It was always good to get away from the big city and breathe some fresh air. Jack would have more opportunities to listen in on cop conversations. He felt pretty sure Ray Ray was Officer Garza's attacker, but he had to be certain before the Can Man met Ray Ray.

Saturday came, and the park was full of police and their families. Many kids running around, wives talking to each other and cops playing catch with their sons. A gentle breeze lifted several colorful kites into the air. The smell of BBQ was making everybody hungry.

Jack brought two lawn chairs and they were sitting under a huge oak tree watching all the kids running after each other.

Jack said, "One day you will be watching your own kids do that."

Heather looked at him and said, "I hope so."

It was a long look. Jack reached for her empty paper plate, put his on top of it and said, "I'll be right back."

As Jack neared the trash can he caught a glimpse of Officer Garza. He was standing near the street and seemed to be in a heated discussion with a heavy-set Hispanic man. This guy looked rough. He had an oily face with pockmarks and a big tattoo on his neck. Jack wondered if he could be Ray Ray.

Their conversation got loud and then Jack heard the big guy yell in Spanish, "*No te voy a dar mas dinero, Garza.*" Even though Jack spoke no Spanish, he did know *dinero* meant money.

All he had to do now was to find out what the rest of the Spanish meant. He had a feeling he knew. The big guy stormed away after yelling at Garza.

On the way back to Heather, Sergeant Mike called to Jack, "Just a moment Jack," with his index finger in the air.

Jack turned around and smiled at Sarg Mike, "Hey, what's up?"

The Sarg asked, "Are you having a good time? That's one beautiful lady you got there."

Jack responded, "Thanks Mike. She's beautiful inside, too. She really makes me happy, and yes, we are having a great time."

Sergeant Mike looked at the ground and said, "I'd like to ask you a question on another subject."

Jack said, "Go ahead, shoot. Ha ha. Not literally."

Sergeant Mike didn't laugh. "You know we at the department really appreciate all that you do for us. I believe your pub helps my men relax a little. It's almost like a pub for cops was no accident."

Jack said, "I feel I can never repay the police for what they did trying to protect my Suzanna."

The Sarg nodded, "Yes, and you know that we consider you one of us. Which by the way brings me to what I want to talk to you about."

Jack looked at Sergeant Mike inquisitively and said, "Okay, what's on your mind?"

The Sarg said, "First of all, this is off the record. I know you must know about Can Man. I figure with so many cops talking around you all the time, you're bound to have heard something."

Jack's smile left his face and said to the Sarg, "To be honest, I have heard bits and pieces. What does this have to do with me?"

Sergeant Mike stepped a little closer to Jack and spoke in a hushed tone, "We at the department are not sure what to think about this guy. I've told my men not to talk about Can Man or to spend their time looking for him. We have plenty of bad guys to look for."

Jack said, "I agree with you."

Sergeant Mike added, "You know it's funny. About the same time, you opened your pub, the Can Man appeared. You also seem to always be trying to care for us cops."

Jack's face went pale.

Mike said, "Like I said before, we're not actively looking for Can Man. If I could say something to Can Man, I would tell him to stop. Thanks, but we can takecare of ourselves."

Jack shook his hand and went back and sat down next to Heather. She had been busy watching the kids play and didn't notice what Jack had seen. A little more time passed and they decided to leave. Jack shook hands with all of his regulars and invited some officers he didn't know to drop in his pub sometime. "Second beer is on the house," he told them in a hushed tone.

A few days later, Jack was at his local supermarket and stopped to talk to the produce guy, Miguel. He was a hard-working guy and always nice to Jack. Actually, Miguel was nice to all the customers. He was sprinkling water on all the veggies, when Jack reached into his pocket to pull out a piece of paper.

He handed it to Miguel and asked, "Miguel, can you translate this?" Jack apologized about the spelling. He just wrote down what it sounded like Ray Ray, or whoever it was, had shouted at Officer Garza.

Miguel looked at the paper and said, "*No te voy a dar mas dinero* means I'm not giving you anymore money." Miguel laughed and said,

"Sounds like somebody doesn't want to give you any more money."

Jack responded, "No, no Miguel. Nobody owes me any money. I just heard it on TV and was wondering what it meant." Jack couldn't very well tell Miguel the truth and the truth was that Ray Ray was a killer of cops...well, an attempted killer of cops, and that was reason enough for Jack. A cop died trying to save his wife's life, and he was going to do everything in his power to see that he saved as many cops' lives as possible.

Starting that night, Jack put on his Can Man outfit and silently walked the tight ropes from building to building, looking down at the dimly lit streets. He found Officer Garza walking his beat. He watched him and had a bird's eye view of everything in front of him and behind him. What Jack was looking for was Ray Ray. Several nights went by and no Ray Ray. Then the night came when it was a little wet after a light sprinkle. Jack saw a dark figure about four blocks in front of Officer Garza.

Jack thought, could *that be Ray Ray?* So, while Garza was stopping to look into store front windows, checking doors and making sure everything was safe and secure, Jack raced ahead and got to a good place to get a better look at the dark figure. Jack pulled out his small but powerful binoculars with a night vision setting. As he zoomed in on the face, he could clearly see it was Ray Ray.

Jack quickly tight-roped back a few buildings to where he thought they would converge. He silently scaled down a fire escape that squeaked a little, but not too much.

As he reached the alley, he found some trash cans against the old brick wall and decided that was a perfect place to hide in plain sight. He squatted down, pulled in his metal slats and lowered his head until he had only a slit to look through. He waited, hoping both men met at the alley entrance. Soon Ray Ray appeared first at the alley and ducked in a little. Jack was looking at Ray Ray when he noticed that he had something in his hand. *Oh no*, Jack thought. Ray Ray had the bush machete. He was there to finish the job.

Officer Garza was nearing the alley. His footsteps could be heard. Ray Ray was barely peeking around the corner. Garza was just steps away, and Ray Ray already had his bush machete raised over his head. Jack thought he couldn't let Garza take a surprise hit.

Just seconds before Garza appeared, Jack pushed over the trash can right next to him. The commotion was very loud. Ray Ray spun around to see where the noise came from. The can scraped against the wall and crashed over.

Garza was in the alley entrance and saw Ray Ray with his bush machete. He went to draw his pistol, but Ray Ray had spun around and hit Garza's arm. He yelled in pain. Ray Ray's back was to the alley and Jack made his move.

He had his special-made throat cutter knife in his right hand. With lightning speed, he thrust his knife under Ray Ray's chin. Ray Ray froze, eyes wide. He dropped his machete. Officer Garza caught his breath and saw what was about to happen. He raised his hand in a halting position and said, "Please stop, Can Man. Please don't kill him."

Jack did stop. Many thoughts were racing through his mind. *His beloved murdered wife Suzanna. His trying to keep the same cops alive and safe who had tried to protect Suzanna. He also thought about his new friendship with Heather. A new beginning, a new chance at life.*

Officer Garza said, "Ray Ray will go to jail. Please lower your knife." Jack decided to lower his special knife. He said nothing. Garza pushed Ray Ray up against the old brick wall there in the alley and was putting on the handcuffs as best he could. While his back was turned, Jack took the opportunity to make his escape. He was already to the top of the four-story building when Garza turned around.

The Can Man was already several buildings away. Jack entered his apartment and took off his Can Man outfit and took a hot shower. He thought maybe he should just give up this protecting the police and turn his attention to his relationship with Heather. Eliminating killers was not going to bring Suzanna back.

Jack had to make a decision. Go through life looking in the rearview mirror at Suzanna or look forward to a life with Heather. He decided he was already helping cops by having a pub where they could meet. As far as Garza taking bribes, well, Jack never intended to be a vigilante trying to take care of the city. He would leave that to others to handle. As he got dried off and looked at his Can Man outfit he thought, *I'm not going to throw you away.*

Jack had a steamer trunk at the end of his bed. He opened it and took out some quilts and blankets. He put the Can Man outfit in and covered it up. As he lay in bed, he looked up at the slowly turning ceiling fan and thought, *I'm going to keep the Can Man outfit just in case.* Because if anybody can help take care of the police, Jack knew he can...man.